DIARY OF A PUG

Pug's Sleepover

By Kyla May

BRANCHES

SCHOLASTIC INC.

D0037404

To my two cats, Bosco and Kobe, who tolerate my three dogs.

Special thanks to Sonia Sander

If you purchased this book without a cover, you should be aware that this book is stolen property. It was reported as "unsold and destroyed" to the publisher, and neither the author nor the publisher has received any payment for this "stripped book."

Art copyright © 2022 by Kyla May
Text copyright © 2022 by Scholastic Inc.

Photos © KylaMay2019

All rights reserved. Published by Scholastic Inc., *Publishers since 1920.* SCHOLASTIC, BRANCHES, and associated logos are trademarks and/or registered trademarks of Scholastic Inc.

The publisher does not have any control over and does not assume any responsibility for author or third-party websites or their content.

No part of this publication may be reproduced, stored in a retrieval system, or transmitted in any form or by any means, electronic, mechanical, photocopying, recording, or otherwise, without written permission of the publisher. For information regarding permission, write to Scholastic Inc., Attention: Permissions Department, 557 Broadway, New York, NY 10012.

This book is a work of fiction. Names, characters, places, and incidents are either a product of the author's imagination or are used fictitiously, and any resemblance to actual persons, living or dead, business establishments, events, or locales is entirely coincidental.

Library of Congress Cataloging-in-Publication Data

Names: May, Kyla, author, illustrator.
Title: Pug's sleepover / by Kyla May.
Description: First edition. | New York, NY : Branches/Scholastic Inc., 2022. | Series: Diary of a pug ; 6 | Summary: Bub the pug and his human Bella plan a pirate-themed sleepover with their friends and discover that even as the best-laid plans go awry they can still have fun.
Identifiers: LCCN 2021001203 (print) | ISBN 9781338713473 (paperback) | ISBN 9781338713480 (reinforced library binding)
Subjects: CYAC: Human-animal relationships–Fiction. | Sleepovers–Fiction. | Pug–Fiction. | Dogs–Fiction. | Diaries–Fiction.
Classification: LCC PZ7.M4535 Pwk 2022 (print) | LCC PZ7.M4535 (ebook) | DDC [Fic]–dc23
LC record available at https://lccn.loc.gov/2021001203
LC ebook record available at https://lccn.loc.gov/2021001204

10 9 8 7 6 5 4 3   22 23 24 25 26

Printed in China 62
First edition, March 2022
Edited by Katie Woehr
Book design by Kyla May and Christian Zelaya

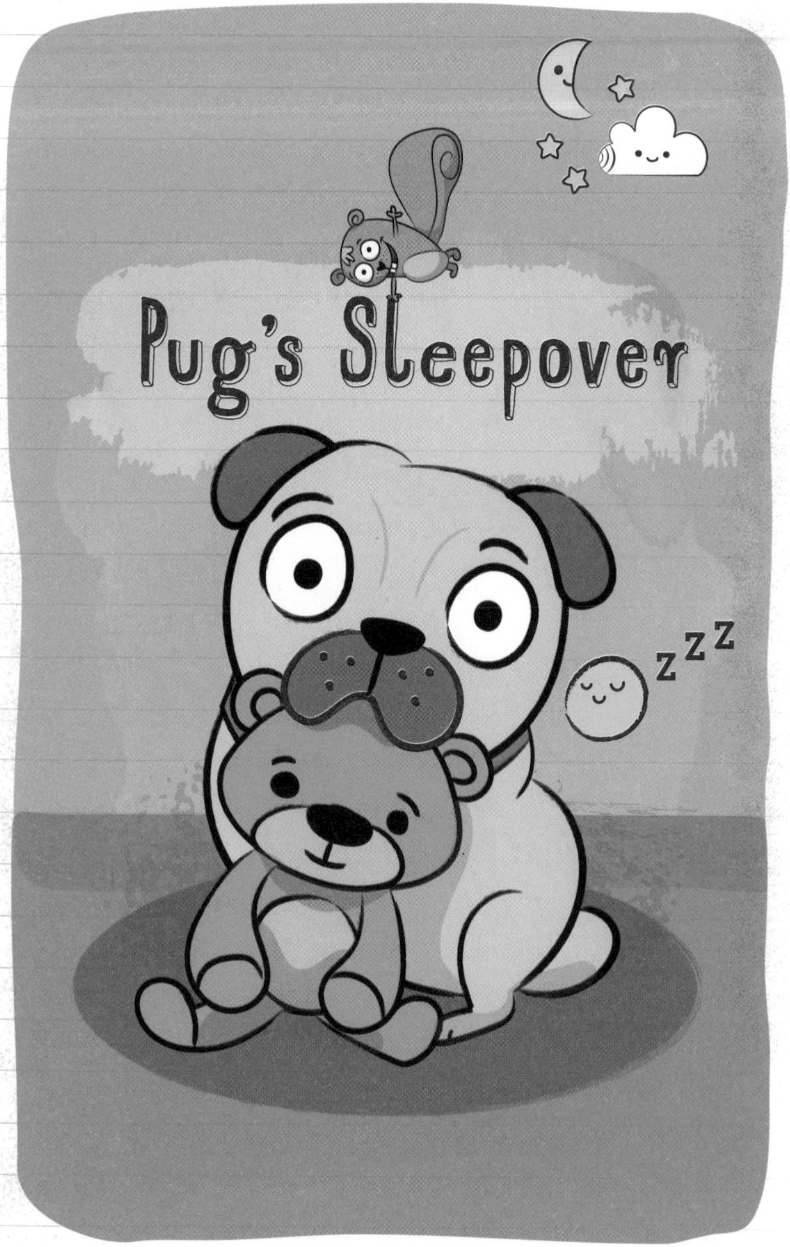
Pug's Sleepover
zzz

Read more Diary of a Pug books!

Table of Contents

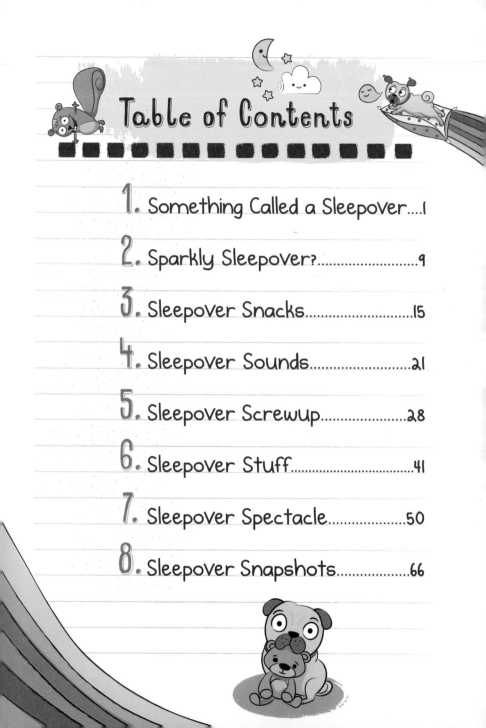

1. Something Called a Sleepover....1

2. Sparkly Sleepover?........................9

3. Sleepover Snacks.........................15

4. Sleepover Sounds.........................21

5. Sleepover Screwup.......................28

6. Sleepover Stuff.............................41

7. Sleepover Spectacle.....................50

8. Sleepover Snapshots.....................66

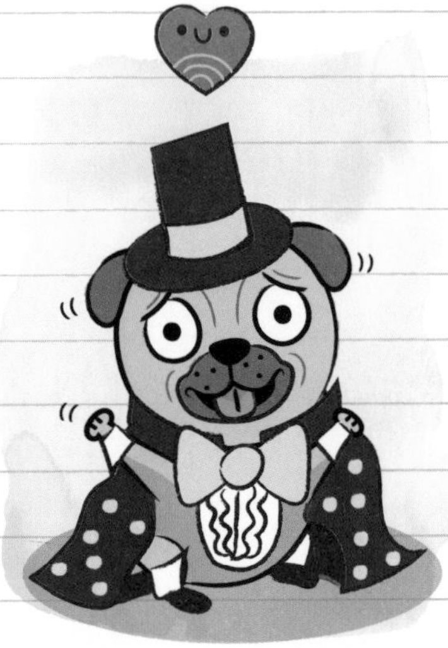

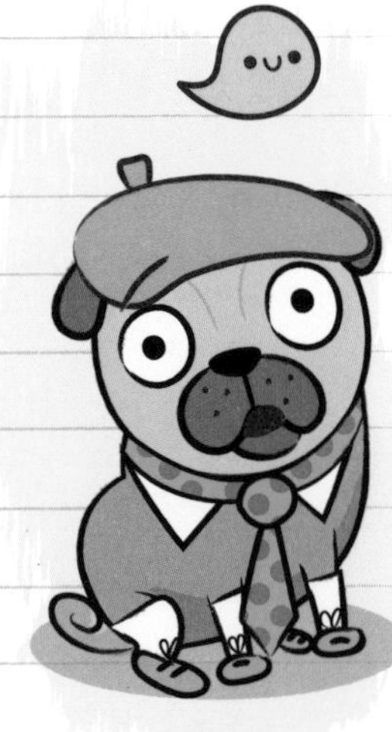

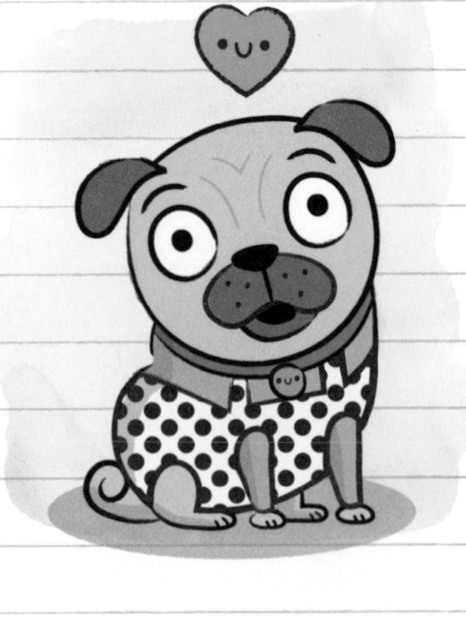

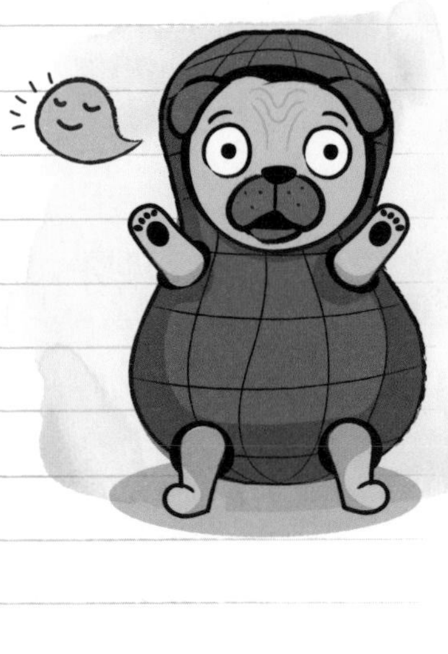

Chapter 1

SOMETHING CALLED A SLEEPOVER

SUNDAY

Dear Diary,

YAWN. It's me, **BUB.**
I'd love a nap. But I have a
story to share!

But first, here are some
things to know about me:

I've got style for miles.

I make many different faces:

Snack Time Face

Need a Nap Face

I'm Sorry Face

These are some of my favorite things:

BEAR

PEANUT BUTTER TREATS

MY BEST FRIEND,
LUNA

Here are some things that get on my nerves:

And **WATER**, of course!

I know it's silly I hate water, because water is how I got my full name, BARON VON BUBBLES. I jumped into a bubble bath when Bella first brought me home. But I didn't know there was WATER under the bubbles!!

Eeeekkk!

BELLA

Now back to my story. Luna and I knew Jack and Bella were planning something.

Uh-oh, Bella has a clipboard.

Maybe she's making a list of how to spoil us!

I liked Luna's thinking. But Bella's lists are always about A PLAN. This list was for something called a "sleepover."

SleepOVER?! I don't like when sleep is OVER.

Spending the night at Jack and Luna's will be fun! Right, Bub?

More time with Jack and Luna IS fun, Diary. But school is out this week and Bella has camp, so I was looking forward to relaxing. That won't happen now! Jack and Luna are going away. So Bella offered to do ALL the planning. (We're having the sleepover when they get back.)

Bella said we'll start planning tomorrow. But what is there to plan? Grab a pillow. Grab Bear. Go to Jack and Luna's house. Sleep! I guess I'll find out what's on Bella's list soon. Good night, Diary.

Chapter 2

SPARKLY SLEEPOVER?

MONDAY

Dear Diary,

Did you know sleepovers have themes sometimes? Bella was trying to think of a theme this morning.

What kind of party should it be, Bub?

RAINBOW PARTY

FROZEN WONDERLAND PARTY

UNDER THE SEA PARTY

I didn't care about the theme. All I cared about was breakfast. But Duchess was blocking my bowl. I growled at her.

Arrrrrrrr.

Is that supposed to scare me?

DOG FOOD

Duchess stayed put. But Bella perked up.

Bub! That's a great idea! "Arrrrr!" We'll have a PIRATE PARTY!

Do pirates get breakfast?

We'll start prepping for the sleepover when I get home from camp. See you later, Bub!

I decided to take a nap while Bella was gone.

Time for some sleepover practice!

Don't you know? No one sleeps at a sleepover.

Says who?

Says me. Before you came along, Bella had a sleepover with her cousins. I hardly slept at all!

I started to worry, Diary. If you don't sleep at sleepovers, what do you do?

When Bella got home, she pulled out the craft supplies.

We need to test out a craft for the sleepover!

Oooh! Are there sparkles?

If there are crafts at sleepovers, I'm in, Diary!

Pirates love parrots. Let's make parrot masks!

Aaa-choo!

I did my best to help Bella make a
sample mask. But most of the feathers
ended up on ME instead of the masks.
Duchess couldn't stop laughing.

All done! What do you think, Bub?

I think I don't like feathers.

SQUAWK!
Does Polly want
a cracker?

Diary, I wish I was captain of a pirate ship right now. I'd make that cat walk the plank.

Chapter 3

SLEEPOVER SNACKS

TUESDAY

Dear Diary,

I woke up to the smell of peanut butter this morning. I raced to the kitchen.

Peanut butter! Best morning ever!

But Bella wouldn't give me any.

This is for later, Bub. Today, we'll be making sleepover snacks: PEANUT BUTTER PIRATE HOOK COOKIES.

Not until I get home, though. So NO TOUCHING these ingredients, okay?

So much for a good morning.

Not eating the ingredients was HARD. In the afternoon, I went outside to distract myself. Nutz showed up.

But guess what? I remembered I DID have treats! A while ago, I hid some for emergencies like this. I told Nutz, "See ya!" and ran back inside.

If I eat these treats, I won't be tempted by Bella's ingredients!

But before I could dig into my treats, Bella came home.

Bubby! Ready to make pirate snacks?

Oh no! I have to stash my secret treats somewhere! Behind this plant will work.

Bella and I made the pirate snacks.

Will you be my official taste tester, Bub?

I thought you'd never ask!

Every batch needed to be tested. Some needed to be tested twice.

You can guess what happened, right?

Oh, Bub, does your tummy hurt?

I never want to eat again.

I left Bella a "gift" in her backpack
before bed.

I felt bad that Bella had to clean up after
me. But those snacks sure were yummy.
Jack and Luna are going to love them!

Chapter 4

SLEEPOVER SOUNDS

WEDNESDAY

Dear Diary,

Today's sleepover prep was something Bella called a "soundscape." She was really getting into the pirate theme. She even talked like a pirate.

Aaarrrr. Methinks we need sound effects. They will add to the pirate feel of the sleepover. Let's record some!

Aye, aye, captain!

We went outside. Bella got some metal things from the garage.

We'll hit this rake and this shovel together. It will sound like pirates sword fighting. Ready to record, matey?

Do I look ready?

Bella pressed record, and we started our "sword fight."

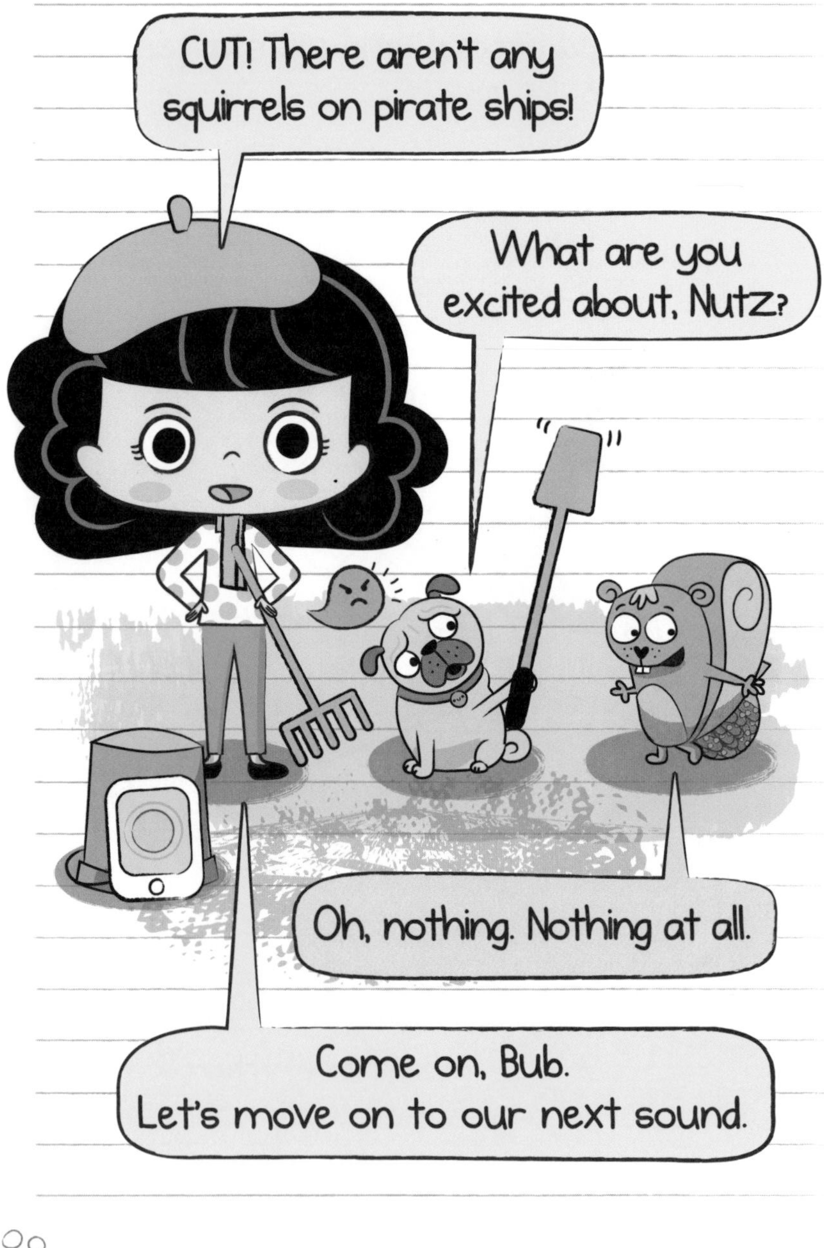
CUT! There aren't any squirrels on pirate ships!
What are you excited about, Nutz?
Oh, nothing. Nothing at all.
Come on, Bub.
Let's move on to our next sound.

We walked to the fountain at the town square to record "ocean sounds." Bella insisted we get really close to the water for the best sound quality.

It's just a little water, Bub.

I'd rather deal with Nutz . . .

I was NOT happy on the wet walk home.

Brrrrr

Don't worry, matey. Our third sound will help you dry off.

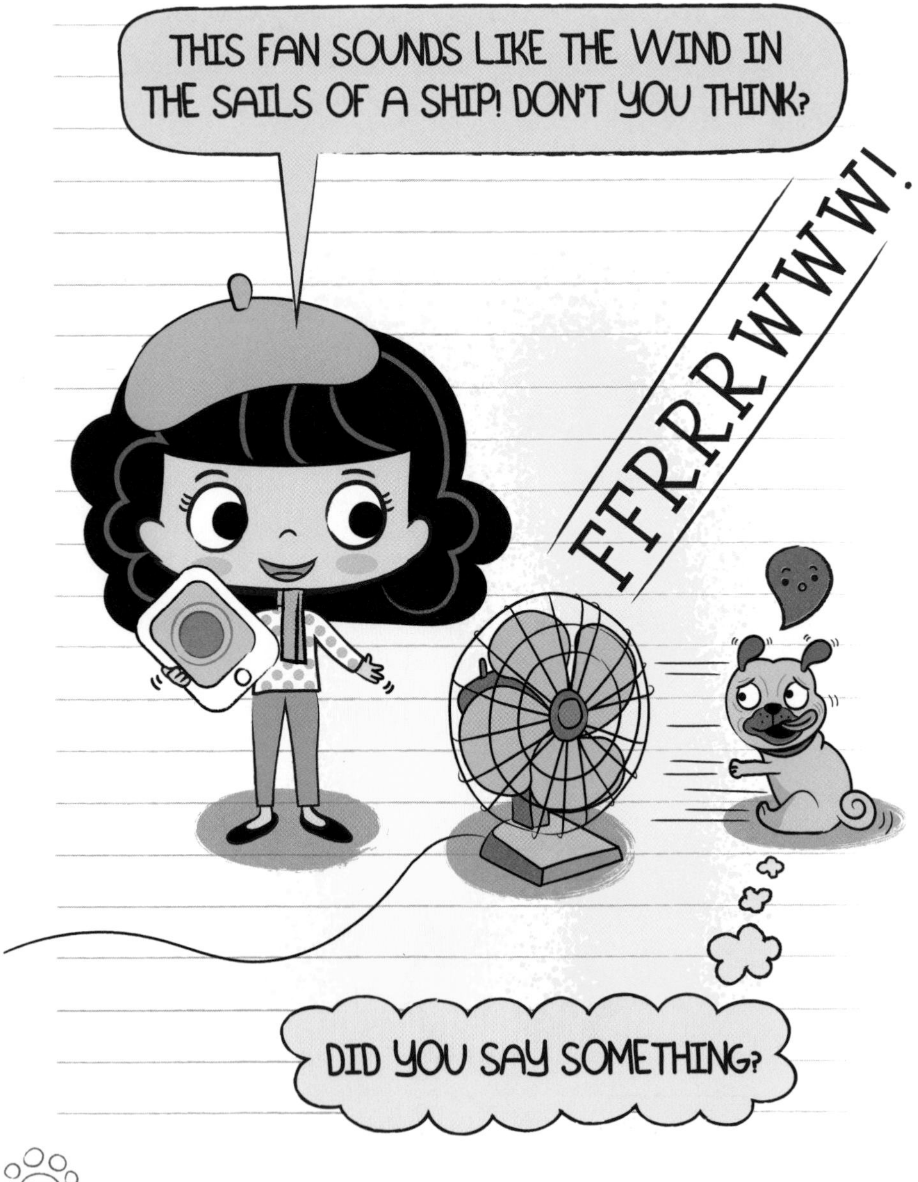
THIS FAN SOUNDS LIKE THE WIND IN THE SAILS OF A SHIP! DON'T YOU THINK?
FFRRRWWW!
DID YOU SAY SOMETHING?

Diary, this soundscape has to be the last item on Bella's sleepover list. What else could there be?

Chapter 5

SLEEPOVER SCREWUP

THURSDAY

Dear Diary,

I woke up late today. I went to the family room and couldn't believe my eyes.

What in the—?!

It was the largest pirate flag I'd ever seen. It was going to look amazing inside Jack's house on Saturday. Bella must have worked hard all morning!

Bella had to leave for camp then.

I'll put everything away when I get home. Don't get into trouble while I'm gone.

No problem. I don't eat pirate flags!

I had a lazy day—my favorite! I napped.

I tried some new outfits.

I napped again.

By afternoon, I was craving a treat. I went to get my secret stash.

GASP! My treats are gone!

I smelled something funny. I followed the smell through my doggy door into the yard . . .

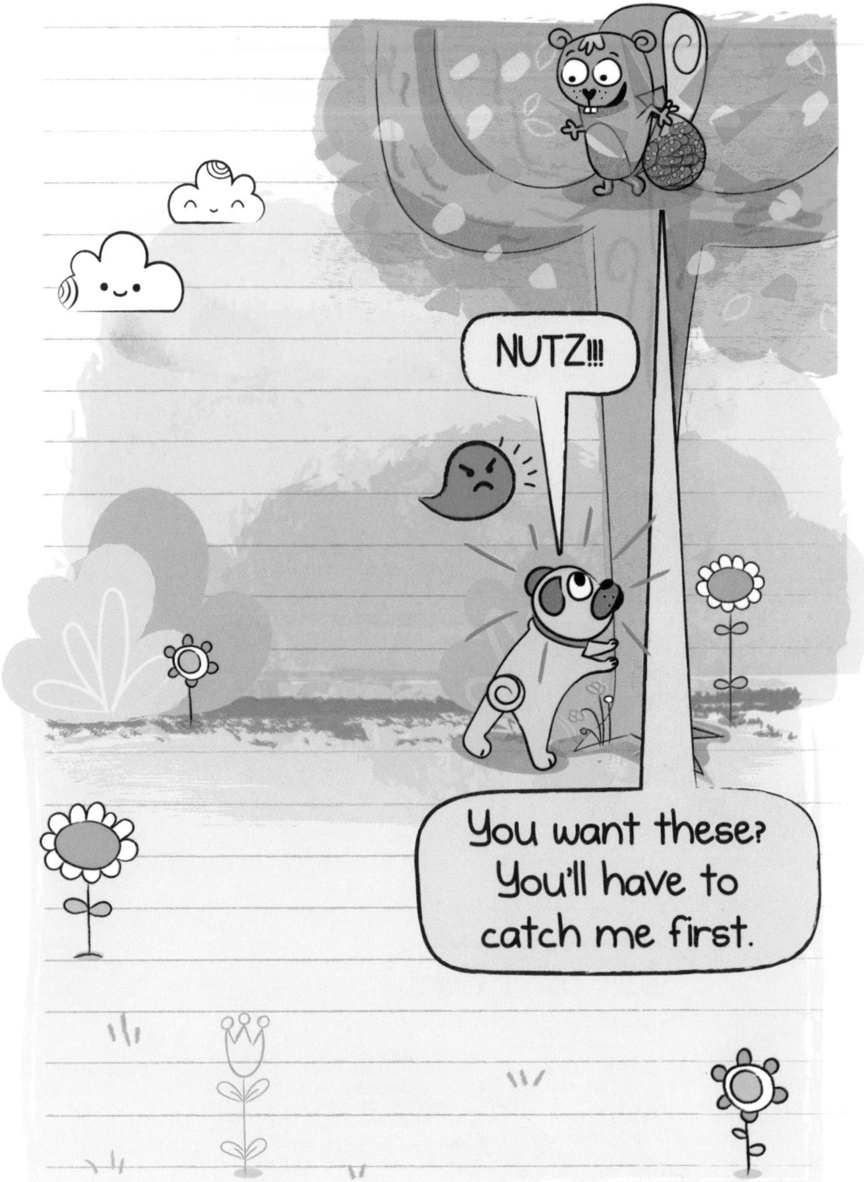
NUTZ!!!
You want these? You'll have to catch me first.

Diary, I chased that squirrel all through the yard.

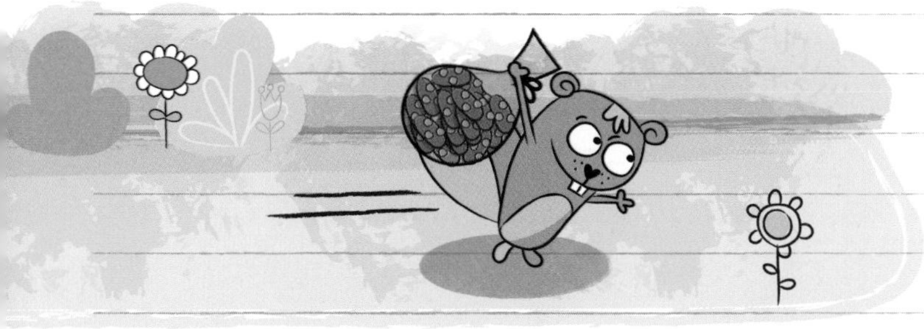

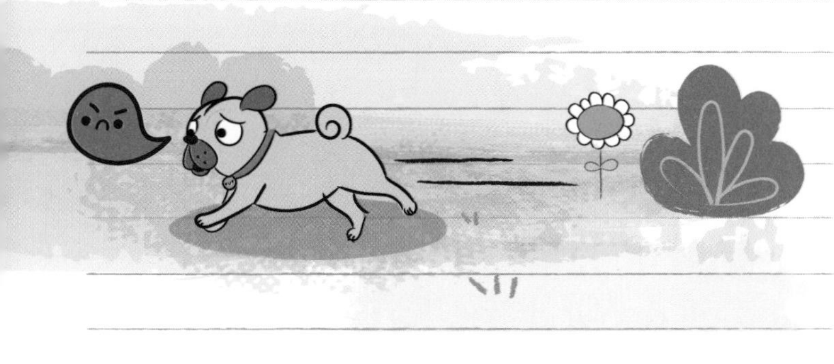

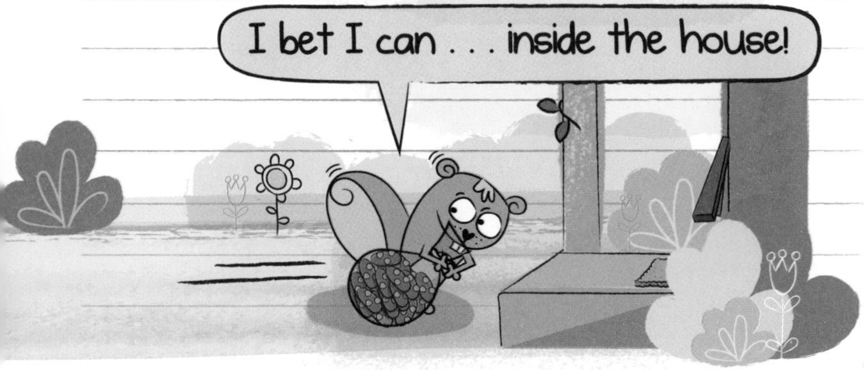
I bet I can . . . inside the house!

Nutz ran through my doggy door. I followed him into the kitchen . . .

. . . and the dining room . . .

. . . and all around the family room.

Just then, we heard the front door.
Bella was home! Nutz dashed out the
window.

When Bella came into the room, she gasped. That's when I realized what a mess Nutz and I had made. The flag was ruined!

I'm sorry.

Bella's mom was mad.

If you don't clean this up by dinnertime, the sleepover is off!

Cancel the sleepover?! Never. I helped Bella clean up fast. We put the flag in the trash. She looked so sad.

Diary, I have to make this up to Bella. But how?

Chapter 6

SLEEPOVER STUFF

FRIDAY

Dear Diary,

After Bella fell asleep last night, I had an idea. I went outside and got the flag pieces from the trash. Nutz showed up.

Need some help?

YOU are offering to help ME?

I heard how upset Bella was. The mess was my fault, too.

I wasn't sure I should trust Nutz. But I realized he could help me make things up to Bella. Squirrels are good at chewing through cardboard.

We made the flag pieces into something new.

I gave him some, Diary. He'd earned them.

I showed Bella the ship when she woke up.

It's awesome, Bub! Better than the flag! You're the best.

Now, today we have to pack. You gather what you need while I'm at camp.

Finally, an easy task!

I put my pillow and Bear by Bella's bag.

Packing done! Nap time!

Bella brought the mail in after camp.

It's a postcard from Jack. He says he has a surprise for us at the sleepover.

Uh-oh! The last surprise from Jack was Luna's high dive for the talent show. I hate water!

But Bella wasn't worried. She started packing.

You can't bring only your pillow and Bear, Bub. We must be prepared.

What else do we need?

Bella made her own pile.

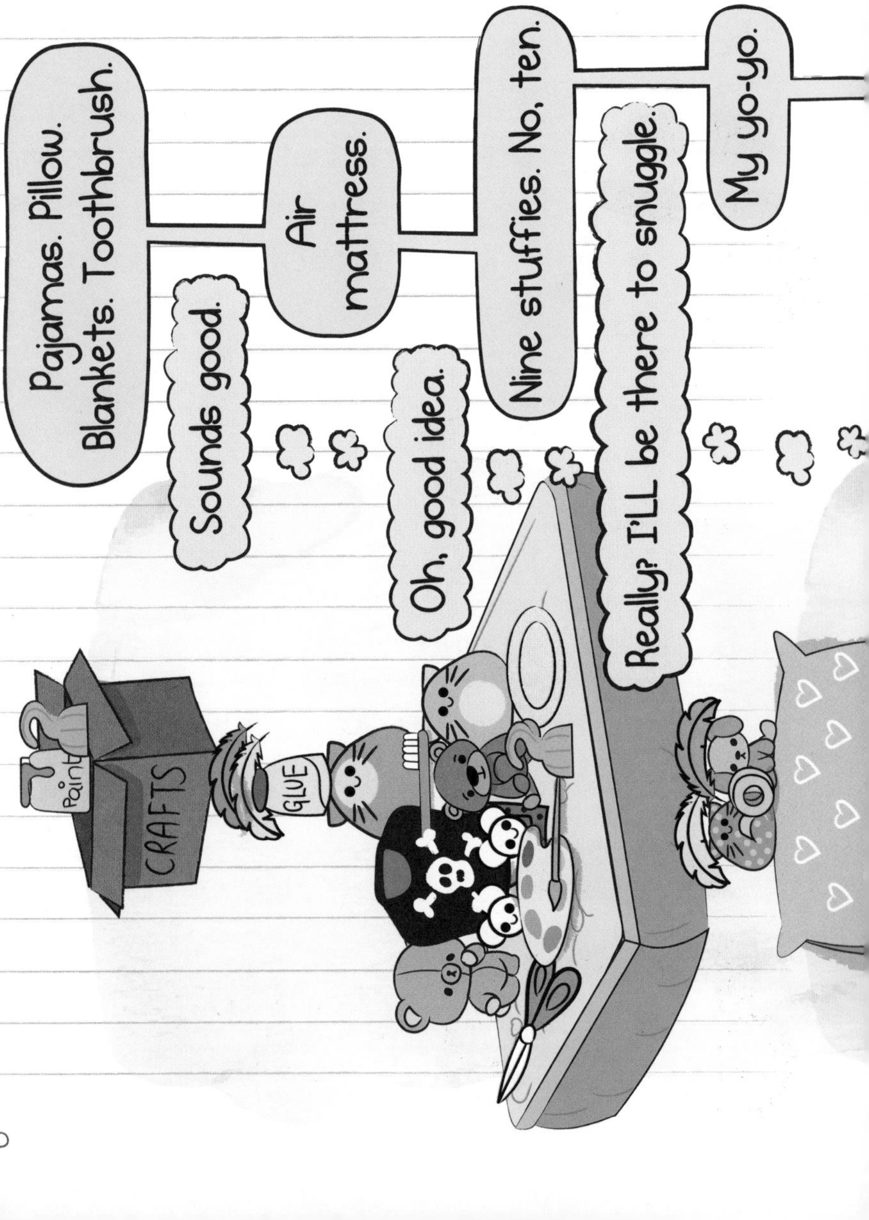

Pajamas. Pillow. Blankets. Toothbrush.
Sounds good.
Air mattress.
Oh, good idea.
Nine stuffies. No, ten.
Really? I'LL be there to snuggle.
My yo-yo.
Paint
CRAFTS
GLUE

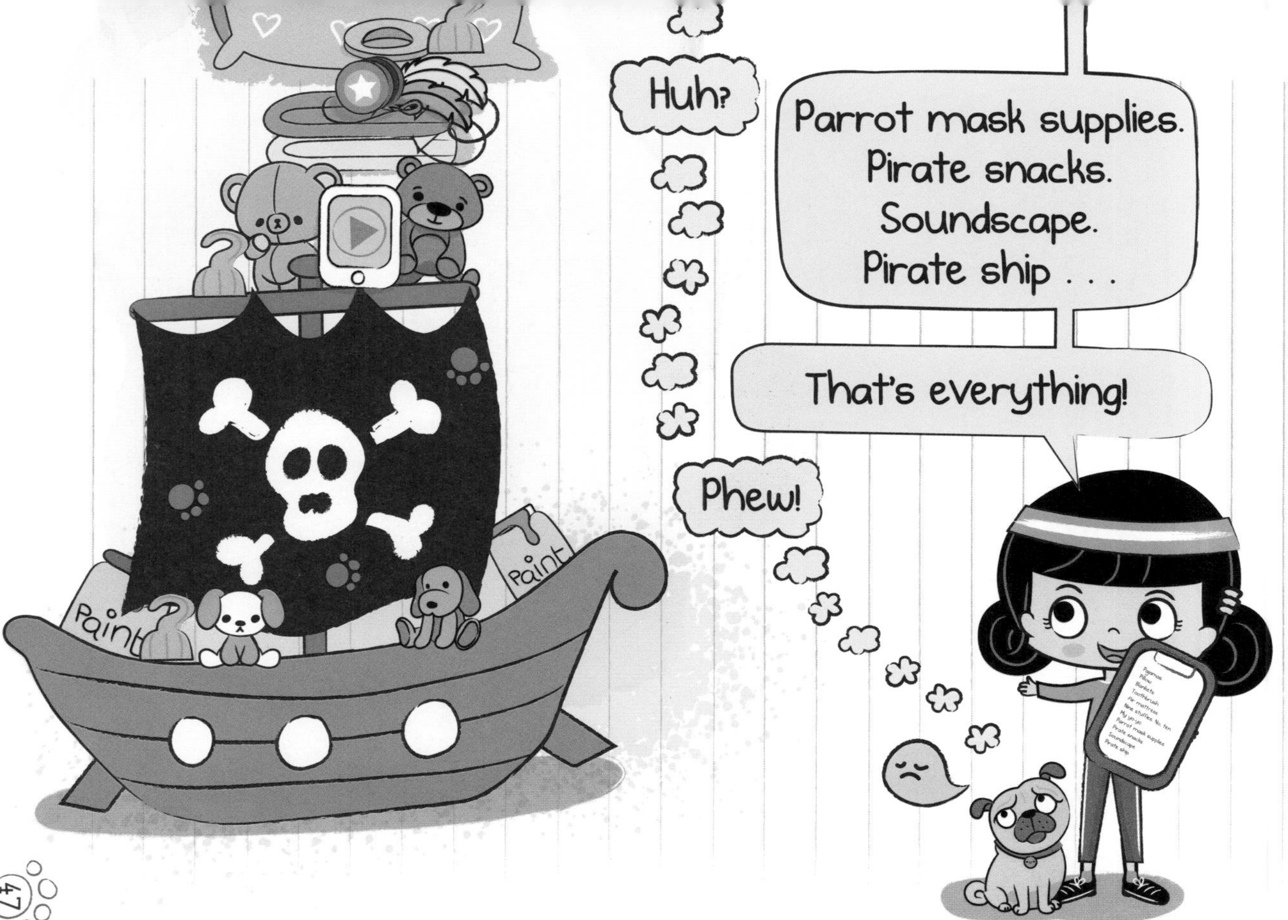
Huh?
Parrot mask supplies.
Pirate snacks.
Soundscape.
Pirate ship . . .
That's everything!
Phew!
Paint
Paint
Pajamas
Pillow
Blankets
Toothbrush
Air mattress
Nine stuffies. No, ten
My yo-yo
Parrot mask supplies
Pirate snacks
Soundscape
Pirate ship

We went to bed, but Bella couldn't sleep.

I can't wait another day for the sleepover, Bub. Let's set up and have our own sleepover in the family room tonight. It will be practice for tomorrow!

That sounded like a lot of work, Diary. But if it made Bella happy . . .

We snuck everything into the family room. Bella hung some blue streamers to look like water and some lights to look like a starry sky.

Thankfully, Diary, at THIS sleepover, we slept. But who knows what will happen tomorrow . . .

Chapter 7

SLEEPOVER SPECTACLE

SATURDAY

Dear Diary,

We packed everything back up this morning.

Today's the day! We'll go to Jack's house after dinner. I wonder what the surprise will be!

Nighttime couldn't come fast enough. Finally, we knocked on Jack's door.

Ahoy, matey! Ready for a pirate sleepover? We'll set this up in your family room—

Come see my surprise first!

Jack led us to the backyard.

We're going to camp out in a tent!

Oh. I . . . I guess that could work.

Bella didn't seem excited about the idea. But she didn't say no.

We put our stuff in the tent.

Wow! You are really prepared.

You can say that again.

Let's get this pirate party started!

Bella wanted to make the parrot masks right away. She showed Jack the sample mask.

We tried to catch the feathers. But the wind got stronger. Bella was sad.

We can't make parrot masks without feathers.

I had to cheer up Bella. But how?

The soundscape! I pressed play. Right away, Bella seemed happier.

All of a sudden, thunder sounded.

BOOM!

Cool sound effect!

That's not on the soundscape . . .

It started to rain. We dashed inside the tent.

But the player wouldn't turn on. It had gotten too wet in the rain.

I pulled on the decorations. That would cheer up Bella.

Yes, Bub! Let's put up the decorations!

And I'll blow up the air mattress.

We set up everything. It was a little crowded when we were done.

It's . . . cozy?

Diary, I think Jack started to wish we were in the house, too.

Jack pointed to the pirate snacks.

Are those for us?

SNACKS

Aye, matey! Let's have some.

We dug in.

Whoa! Luna! Easy—you're getting crumbs all over.

All of a sudden, Bella screamed.

The ants were almost gone when we heard another sound. Jack shouted. Luna jumped. The snacks went flying.

der boomed again. Luna FREAKED

That was it, Diary. Nobody was having fun.
I had to do something.

I stuck my head outside the tent. The rain soaked me, but I needed to save this sleepover. I grabbed my pillow and Bear. I barked to get everyone's attention. Then I dashed out into the rain toward the house. I just hoped everyone would follow . . .

Chapter 8

SLEEPOVER SNAPSHOTS

SUNDAY

Dear Diary,

Luckily, everyone ran inside after me last night.

Jack's mom gave us blankets.

We didn't do any crafts, but we told jokes.

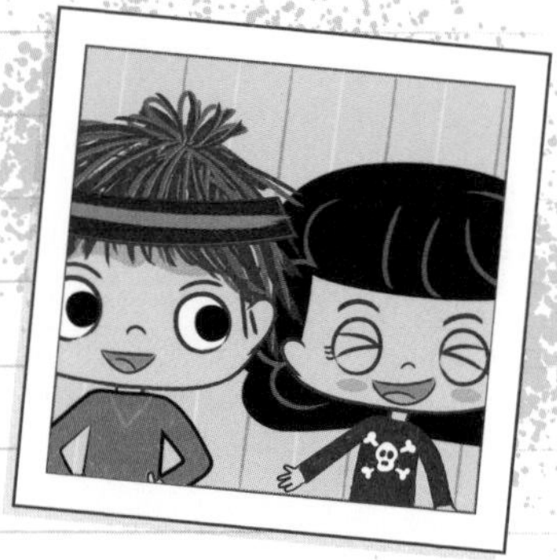

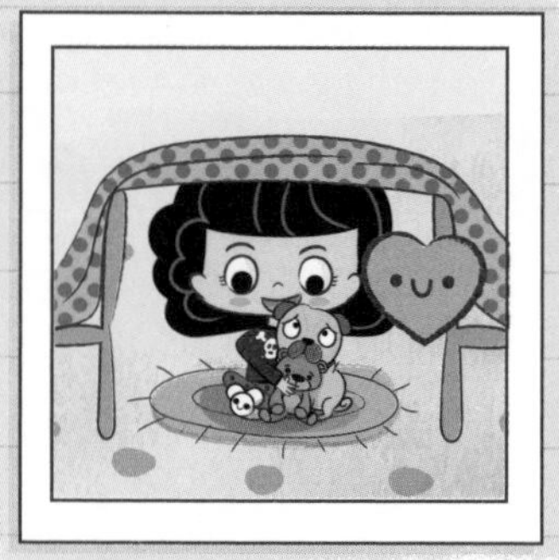

We made our own kind of tent.

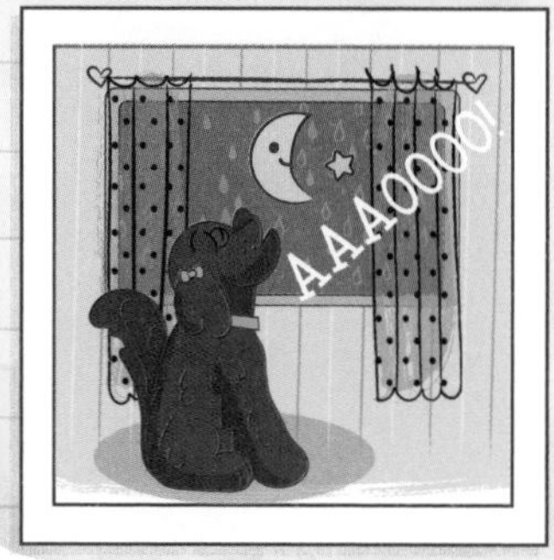
AAAOOOO!

We listened to a soundscape of sorts.

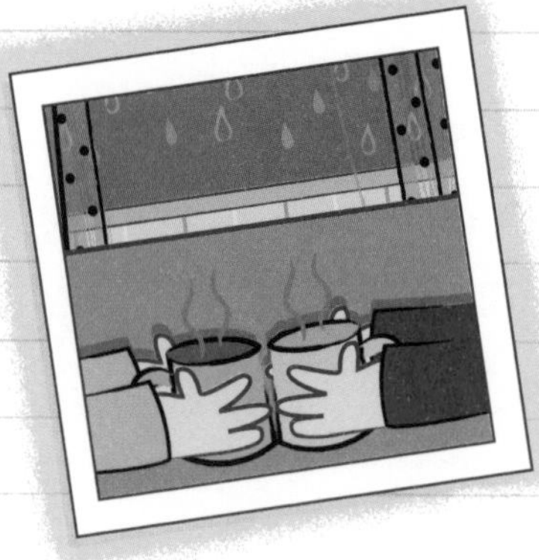

Jack's mom made hot chocolate.

We even had an epic yo-yo contest.
(I lost.)

We didn't have a theme, or decorations,
or a pile of supplies. But we had one
another.

I remembered what Duchess told me
earlier—that no one sleeps at sleepovers.
She was right! We had too much fun to
sleep!

In the morning, we went outside. Our tent was flat. So was the air mattress.

Look! That hissing noise wasn't a snake. It was air coming out of the mattress. We must have made a hole when we stomped away the ants.

But . . . if there wasn't a snake, what's that slithering under the tent?

Diary, something was definitely moving under the tent. Then I heard a sound I knew all too well . . .

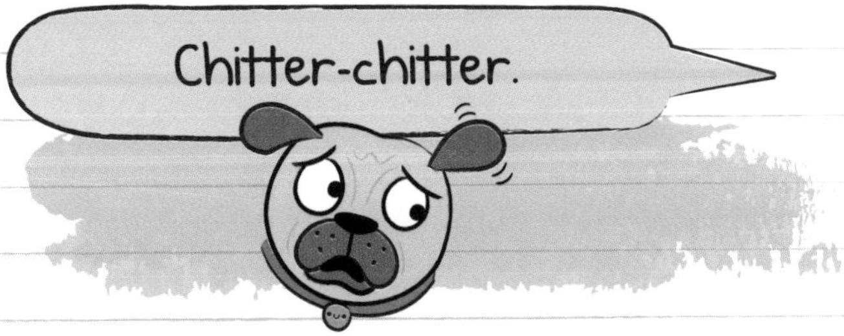
Chitter-chitter.

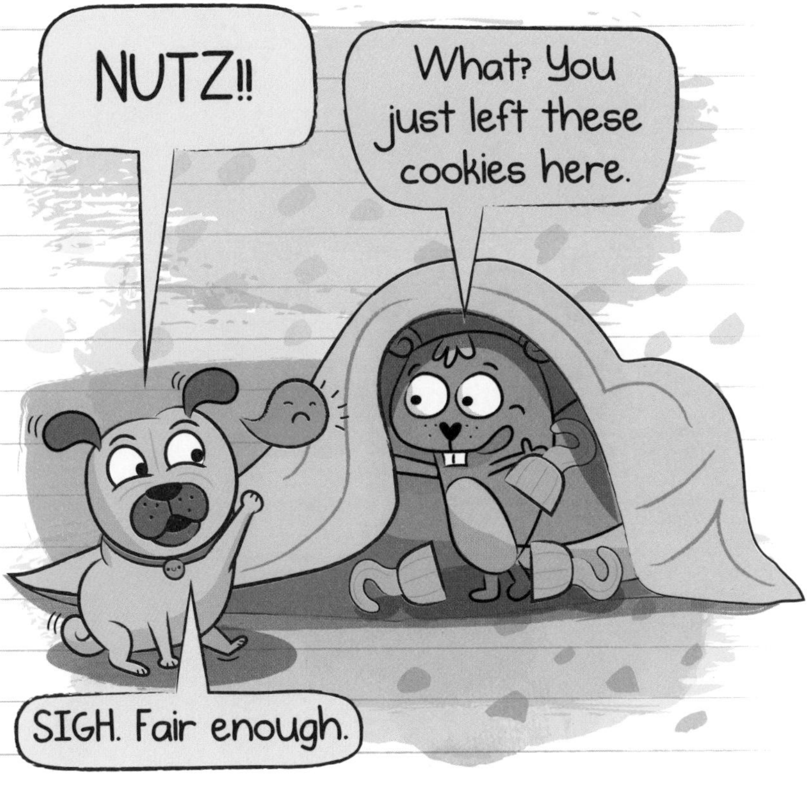
NUTZ!!
What? You just left these cookies here.
SIGH. Fair enough.

We said goodbye to Jack and Luna and went back home. Bella's already planning our next sleepover. Me? I'll see you later, Diary. I'm off to take an epic nap.

What should our next theme be, Bub? Outer space?

Spacing out sounds good to me!

Kyla May is an Australian illustrator, writer, and designer. In addition to books, Kyla creates animation. She lives by the beach in Victoria, Australia, with her three daughters and two dogs. The character of Bub was inspired by her daughter's pug called Bear.

HOW MUCH DO YOU KNOW ABOUT DIARY OF A PUG

Pug's Sleepover?

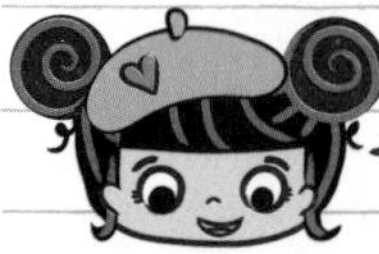

What gives me the idea for a pirate theme? Re-read page 10.

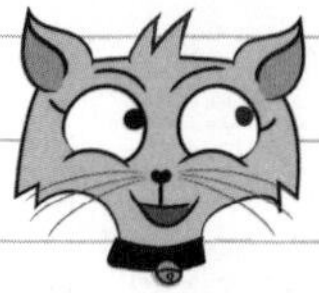

What do I tell Bub about sleepovers that worries him? Re-read page 11.

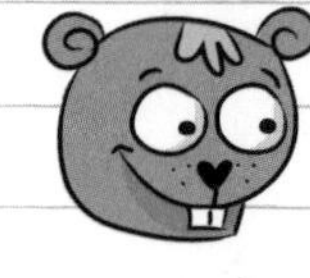

When Bub talks like a pirate and says, "aye, aye, captain!" what does he mean? Re-read page 21.

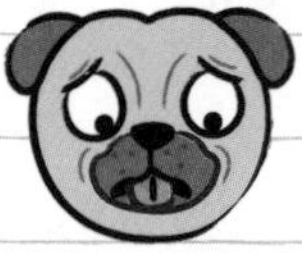

When no one is having fun at the sleepover, neither Bella nor Jack says how they're feeling. Have you ever not wanted to tell a friend something? Why didn't you want to speak up?

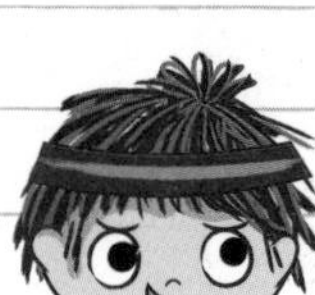

If you were having a sleepover, what would your theme be? Draw what your decorations would look like.

scholastic.com/branches